Jungle Shorts

IRENE RAWNSLEY

Illustrated by Tony Kerins

dingles & company

First published in the United States of America in 2008 by
dingles & company
P.O. Box 508
Sea Girt, New Jersey 08750

First Printing

Website: www.dingles.com
E-mail: info@dingles.com

Library of Congress Catalog Card Number
2007906262

ISBN
978-1-59646-858-0 (library binding)
978-1-59646-859-7 (paperback)

Jungle Shorts
Text © Irene Rawnsley, 1995
This U.S. edition of *Jungle Shorts*, originally published in English in
1995, is published by arrangement with Oxford University Press.

The moral rights of the author have been asserted.
Database right Oxford University Press (maker).

Printed in China

It was Friday afternoon. Mr. Cox's class had put on their coats and were waiting in line to go home. Lenny was at the back because the zipper on his jacket had stuck. He was so busy with the zipper that he nearly missed what Mr. Cox said.

"Here's a letter for you all," said Mr. Cox. "Don't lose it, and don't forget to give it to your parents. There's good news inside."

Lenny wanted to know what the good news was. He rushed across the playground to meet his mom.

"Quick! Open this letter," he said.
"Mr. Cox says there's good news inside."

"Say hello to me first!" laughed his
mom, but she opened the letter. She
read it and told him, "Your class is
having soccer lessons. Next week. The
school will lend you some shoes."

"Wow!" shouted Lenny. "Real soccer! I bet I score fifteen goals!"

His mom put the letter in her bag.

"What about a striped shirt and socks? Can I have a real soccer shirt?" begged Lenny.

"Wait and see," said Mum.

At home, Lenny couldn't get out of his jacket and his mom had to help him.

"I'm glad you didn't break the zipper. I can't get you another jacket until next month," she said.

"I don't want a new jacket," said Lenny, "but can I have a real soccer shirt? Please?"

"Ask me after your snack," said his mom.

Lenny had leftover pancakes with apples and jam. Leftover pancakes were Lenny's favorite snack treat. But today he ate as fast as he could.

He put down his knife and fork with a clatter.

"You promised to talk about soccer things after my snack," he said.

Mom took Mr. Cox's letter from
her bag.

"Each child will need an old T-shirt
and some socks," she read.

"No real soccer things?" asked Lenny.

"I'm sorry, no. Except for shorts.
Mr. Cox wants you all to have new
shorts. We'll go to the marketplace
tomorrow to look for some."

Lenny was not happy, but he knew his mom. She had made up her mind, and that was that. He looked at his photos of soccer stars. They looked great. "I bet they always wore a real soccer shirt," he thought. "I bet they didn't have to wear an old T-shirt."

That night he lay awake thinking. He was going to make sure his mom bought soccer shorts. He wanted *real* white soccer shorts. Then he knew he could score lots of goals.

2

After breakfast the next day, they set out to buy the new shorts. The marketplace was two streets away from where Lenny lived. On the way they saw Ted and Shane from Mr. Cox's class. Ted and Shane lived near Lenny. They were kicking a ball back and forth.

Shane slammed the ball over to him, and Lenny kicked it back.

"Want to play?" called Ted.

"I can't, not now. I'm going to buy new soccer shorts with my mom."

"We've got ours already," Ted shouted back.

The marketplace was very crowded. Everyone was looking at the fruit and vegetables piled high in the stalls. There were shoes and clothes for sale under striped canvas roofs. One man was selling shorts.

"Get your jungle shorts!" he shouted.

He was wearing a wide straw hat and an enormous pair of jungle shorts over his pants. They had big green trees on them with monkeys smiling at the top.

"Big or small, they don't cost much," said the man.

"No thanks," said Lenny. "I'm going to start soccer lessons next week. I need real soccer shorts."

He pulled at his mom's hand. They struggled through the crowds trying to find real soccer shorts. They found lots of shorts that were too big and a little white pair that was too small. When they did find a pair in Lenny's size, they cost far too much money.

"We'll just have to get the jungle shorts," said Mom. "The colors are fun. I'm sure you'll like them better than white ones."

Lenny made a face. "Oh, Mom!" he said. "But – "

"No buts," said his mom.

They went slowly back to the man selling jungle shorts. The pile in his stall had gone down a lot.

"I knew you'd come back. I put aside a pair just for you," said the man.

He held a pair of jungle shorts against Lenny's pants.

"A perfect fit!" he said with a smile.

Lenny's mom opened her purse and paid for the shorts. The man put them in a bag and handed it over.

"There you are, son. Have fun wearing them!"

Lenny did not smile. "I wish they were real soccer shorts," he said.

"Jungle shorts are the next best thing," said his mom.

On the way home they saw Tessa
and Pam from Mr. Cox's class kicking a
ball against a fence. They lived on
Lenny's street.

"We can't wait till Monday for
soccer," said the girls. "We've got
new shorts!"

"So have I," said Lenny. But he
didn't open his bag to show them.

3

On Monday afternoon, the class was
waiting for its first soccer lesson.
Everybody was noisy and excited,
swinging their bags of soccer things.
Lenny was at the back with the jungle
shorts in his bag. He didn't want to put
them on.

Mr. Cox carried a big box of shoes
into the changing rooms. They spent
a long time finding shoes to fit
everyone.

"Now, put on your soccer things
and be quick about it," he said.

Lenny wished he could sneak out
the door and go home.

When they were all ready, Mr. Cox shouted, "Get in line, everyone!"

Lenny made sure he was at the back again. He didn't want anybody to see his jungle shorts, and he hid behind Ted. When he looked down to see what Ted was wearing, he got a big surprise.

Ted was wearing jungle shorts, too! Lenny nudged him in the back and said, "Your shorts are the same as mine!"

"Yes," said Ted, "and the same as Pam's and Tessa's and Shane's!"

It was true. All the friends from
Lenny's street were wearing jungle
shorts. Mr. Cox smiled.

"Five children in the same shorts.
It must be a record!" he said

"And we all live on Lyon Street,"
said Lenny.

"In that case you should all play for
the same team. You can be the Lyon
Street Lions."

When Mr. Cox had picked three more teams, they went out to the playing field.

They played soccer until it was time to go home. The Lions beat all the others, and Mr. Cox said they were the champions. Lenny scored five goals.

In the changing rooms the children took off their muddy shoes and put on their clothes.

"All uniforms must be washed and shoes clean for next Monday," said Mr. Cox. "Don't leave it for your mom. Do it as soon as you get home and then you won't forget."

Lenny was the first to be ready, and he ran to meet his mom at the gate. He told her about his five goals and the Lyon Street Lions.

"We'd better go home quickly now," said Lenny. "I have to clean my shoes and wash my shorts!"

And when Mr. Cox drove home for dinner later on, he smiled to himself. On Lyon Street there were five pairs of jungle shorts blowing on the washing lines.

About the author

Ever since I was little, I've always liked writing poems and stories. Nowadays, I write in a room overlooking fields and hills, and I'm often joined by our black-and-white cats, Silver and Fagley. Fagley was an  abandoned kitten, and he was named after the first bus that passed us on the way home.

My own children are grown-up now, but I have two grandsons, Luke and Peter, who take a great interest in my books.